It's About Ti
Jesse Bear

and Other Rhymes

by Nancy White Carlstrom

illustrated by Bruce Degen

SCHOLASTIC INC.

New York Toronto London Auckland Sydney

No part of this publication may be reproduced in whole or in part, or
stored in a retrieval system, or transmitted in any form or by any means,
electronic, mechanical, photocopying, recording, or otherwise, without
written permission of the publisher. For information regarding permission,
write to Macmillan Publishing Company, 866 Third Avenue,
New York, NY 10022.

ISBN 0-590-45421-8

Text copyright © 1990 by Nancy White Carlstrom.
Illustrations copyright © 1990 by Bruce Degen.
All rights reserved. Published by Scholastic Inc., 730 Broadway, New York,
NY 10003, by arrangement with Macmillan Publishing Company.

12 11 10 9 8 7 6 5   3 4 5 6 7/9

Printed in the U.S.A.   09

First Scholastic printing, September 1992

For my editor, Judith Whipple,
and my niece, Rebecca Jean White —
two Jesse Bear fans.
— N.W.C.

For everybody at E.R. Murrow,
but especially Laurel.
— B.D.

It's About Time!

Tiptoe! Tiptoe!
Listen at the door.
Mama! Papa!
Early morning snore.

Two big bumps
Underneath the covers,
Papa is one
Mama is the other.

Wake up! Wake up!
Open up your eyes.
Guess what! Guess what!
Superbear can fly.

Two big growls
Underneath the covers,
Papa is one
Mama is the other.

Tiptoe! Tiptoe!
Quiet Superbear.
Whisper! Whisper!
What's under there?

Two big bears
Throwing off their covers,
Papa is one
Mama is the other!

Laughing! Laughing!
Feeling mighty fine.
Get up! Get up!
It's about time!

Three big sillies
Dancing under cover
Papa, Mama
Jesse is the other.

Dressing Myself Today

I'm dressing myself
Yes, I'm dressing myself
I'm dressing myself today.

I'll put on my pants
That are covered with stars,
My jeans with the hole
and my shirt with the cars.

I'll put on suspenders
And red and white socks,
My brown leather vest
And a hat from my box.

A belt with a buckle
A dinosaur pin,
Not ready quite yet
I'll start over again.

I'll put on my shorts
And my Superbear cape,
Broken sunglasses
Mended with tape.

An old tie of Papa's
And Mama's old sash,
I've been dressing myself
And I'm finished at last.

I've been dressing myself
Yes, dressing myself
I've been dressing myself today.

Cubby Crunchies

Cubby Crunchies
Great to eat
With milk and honey—
What a treat!

I shake the box
And look inside—
Cubbies rumble
Tumble slide.

Cubby Crunchies
All fall down,
Land in my bowl
Blue and round.

But the Cubbies'
Best surprise
Is when they come out
With a prize.

Boxes Are Best

Slide it, ride it
Climb inside it.

Boxes are best for Jesse Bear.

Stack up, sprawl out
Duck down, crawl out.

Boxes are best for Jesse Bear.

City of skyscrapers
Houses with flowers
Tunnels and bridges
Airport with towers.

Drum on, strum on
New toys are fun
But the boxes they come in are best.

Oh yes!

Boxes are best
Boxes are best

Boxes are best for Jesse Bear.

Hurry! Hurry!

You say, Hurry Jesse! Hurry Jesse!
Late! Late! Late!
I say, Please Mama! Please Mama!
Wait! Wait! Wait!

You say, Hurry Jesse! Hurry Jesse!
Go! Go! Go!
I say, Can't Mama! Can't Mama!
No! No! No!

You say, What Jesse? What Jesse?
Why? Why? Why?
I say, Slow Mama! Slow Mama!
Try! Try! Try!

You say, Right Jesse! Right Jesse!
Time! Time! Time!
I say, Thanks Mama! Thanks Mama!
Fine! Fine! Fine!

The Puddle Song

Boots squish down
In the soft brown mud
Muck-stuck, muck-stuck
Pull and tug.

Pull and tug
Pull and tug
Squish a song
Of sticky mud.

Boots wash off
In the puddle bay
Slip-drip, slip-drip
Splash and play.

Splash and play
Splash and play
Drip a song
Of puddle bay.

Play it wet
And play it long
Play a muddle-puddle song.

Favorite Flower

Flowers in a bed
Flowers in a row
Flowers on the fence
Watch them grow.

Some stand tiny
Some stand tall
Some hang over
And others crawl.

Bee flowers
Tree flowers
Flowers on a vine

Flowers in the morning
Flowers all the time.

Yellow flowers
Orange flowers
Purple, red and blue.

I pick my favorite flower
And give it to you.

Nitty Gritty Sand Song

Sing a song of mud pies
Bake a puddle cake
Leaf and branches sandwich
Easy food to make.

When the meal is ready
All the ants will come
Nitty gritty party
They'll take home the crumbs.

Nitty gritty music
Nitty gritty dance
Nitty gritty sand song
Don't take home the ants!

Yum! Yum!

Oranges are juicy
Oranges are sweet
Yum, these oranges
Are good to eat.

Peel a banana
Break in three pieces
Mash it and smash it
Oh, how delicious.

Peanut butter
And jelly too
On crackers and bread
What wonderful goo.

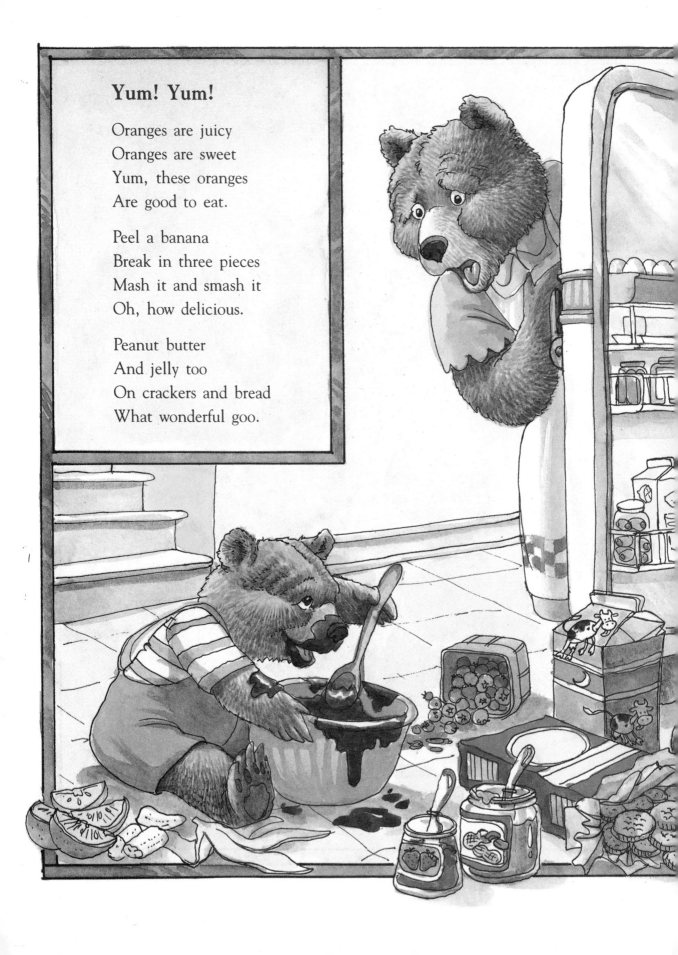

Milk is gurgly
Milk is sippy
Milk makes puddles
White and drippy.

Blueberries squish
Apples crunch
Tomatoes slip and slide
For lunch.

Rice is nice
For raining down
But pudding is best
For messing around.

Sprouts!

I love alfalfa sprouts.
Some wiggle in
Some jiggle out.
They add a little flavor
They add a little munch
Growing on my sandwich
In a great green bunch.

Dance of the Goldfish

You haven't any toes
And you haven't any feet,
But you dance through the water
To the Goldfish Beat.

With a wiggle and a waggle
And a flip and a flail,
You shimmy through the water
Tippy-toes on your tail.

Do the shimmy-swimmy!

Do the flash-splash!

With a shiver and a quiver
And a slap and a splash,
You shine through the water
With a Goldfish Flash.

You haven't any toes
And you haven't any feet,
But you dance through the water
To the Goldfish Beat.

No More Medicine

No more medicine
No more, no more today
I feel like getting up
I know I am okay.

No more medicine
It really makes me sick
I mean, I'm getting better
This medicine is quick.

No more medicine
No gooey, bright pink stuff
No more medicine
I'm sure I've had enough.

No more medicine
No more, no more today
Well, maybe just a spoonful
Then I'll go out to ----

Zzz! Zzz! Zzz!

It's About Time, Jesse Bear

Now I lay me down to sleep
Bear angels at my head and feet.
When I close my eyes real tight
As you turn off my spaceman light
(No more stories, no more songs)
When I sleep the whole night long,
What will you say as I sleep there?

It's about time, my Jesse Bear!

And then I'll kiss you just once more
I'll listen for "Don't close the door."
I will not be at all surprised
When you open up your eyes.
I'll know you're not asleep for sure
When I hear you say "One more."

One more story
One more rhyme
One more kiss
And now, it's time!

Good-night.